foxy
feels unwell

This edition first published in Great Britain by HarperCollins*Publishers* Ltd in 2001

1 3 5 7 9 10 8 6 4 2

ISBN: 0 00 664758 8

The HarperCollins website address is:
www.fireandwater.com

Printed by Printing Express Limited, Hong Kong

foxy
feels unwell

Colin and Jacqui Hawkins

Collins

An imprint of HarperCollinsPublishers

There was something the matter with Foxy.

SIGH!

But what was it?

"Come on, Foxy," said his little sister.

"Let's play outside."

"No!" said Foxy.

At supper time it was Foxy's favourite – beans on toast.
"YUK!" said Foxy.

"Do you want to read a book?" said his little sister.
"No!" moaned Foxy. "Go away."

"Let's play with your cars," said his little sister.
"Don't want to," said Foxy.
"How about a jigsaw?"
"NO!" shouted Foxy.

KICK!
CRUNCH!

"I don't want to do ANYTHING!"

PHEW!

Foxy didn't feel well.

"What's the matter?" asked his little sister.

"I don't know," moaned Foxy. "My head aches, I'm hot and I'm going to bed!"

Foxy's little sister helped him get ready for bed.
Soon Foxy was fast asleep.

The next morning, Foxy had a surprise.
ITCH! ITCH! SCRATCH! SCRATCH!

"You're all spotty," said Foxy's little sister.
Foxy had CHICKEN POX.
"I'll look after you," said his little sister.
But Foxy just groaned.

Foxy's little sister looked after Foxy very well.

She tucked him up, she read him a story and she brought him a cold drink.

Foxy started to feel better.

"I want to play with my toys now," he said.

"Watch this!"

"Don't want to," said his little sister.

"I'm hungry!" said Foxy. "Time for breakfast."

"I feel sick!" said his little sister.

"Let's go outside and play," said Foxy.

"I don't want to!" said his little sister.

"Come on!" said Foxy.

"I DON'T WANT TO!" yelled his little sister.

CLATTER! CLATTER!

"Stop it!" said Foxy. "What's the matter?"

Just then the doorbell rang. RING! RING!

It was Badger and Dog.

"Hallo!" said Badger. "We're spotty!"

"We're all spotty!" said Dog.

"My little sister's not spotty," said Foxy.

"Come on, let's play."

"No!" yelled Foxy's little sister, "LEAVE ME ALONE!"

"What's the matter with your little sister?"
said Badger.
"Dunno," said Foxy. "She doesn't want
to do anything."

"WHEE! Let's play spotty football!"
shouted Dog.
And the three friends played all afternoon.

At teatime they had spotty cake, but
Foxy's little sister didn't want any.
"What's wrong?" asked Badger.
"LOOK!" she said. "SPOTS!"

"Now we're all spotty," laughed Foxy.
"And it's my turn to look after you!"